BEAVER

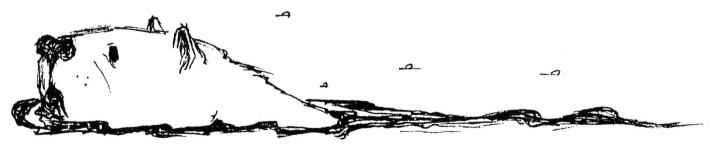

GLEN ROUNDS

BEAVER

Holiday House / New York

The beaver is well known for his habit of building dams and cutting down trees with no tools but his paws and sharp teeth.

On dry land he is somewhat clumsy and slow moving.

But his wide, flat tail and webbed
hind feet make him a powerful
swimmer, and he does much of
his work underwater.

So he likes to live and do his work
in deep ponds, where he can
swim from place to place safe
from enemies on the banks.

If a beaver moves into a neighborhood where there is no pond, he soon sets out to make one by building a dam across some small stream.

This first small dam grows slowly, but whenever he finds the backed-up water running around or over it, the beaver piles on more dead branches, mud, and trash.

As he builds the dam higher and longer, the water behind it grows deeper, and in a few weeks there is a deep new pond where there had been none before.

The beaver is a night worker, and
during the day, while the wood
ducks, herons, and other
neighbors go about their
business, he stays sound
asleep in his den.

But in late afternoon or early evening, he wakens and comes out to float quietly awhile, listening for danger.

If he hears nothing to disturb him, he soon swims off to find something to eat.

Beavers are vegetarians and eat
many kinds of water plants and
roots they find along the edges
or the bottom of the pond.

But the main part of a beaver's diet is bark from trees.

Holding a small branch in his paws, a beaver will gnaw off the green bark like a man eating corn off the cob.

To get at the bark on high branches, the beaver will cut down even a tall tree by gnawing away chips from its base until it falls.

The beaver may do some chores during the night—repairing his dam, cutting down trees—things like that.

But between jobs he spends most of his time swimming from place to place, looking for food.

When daylight comes, he stops whatever he is doing and swims toward his lodge, or one of his bank burrows.

He may stop for a snack or two on the way, but by sunrise he will have dived through one of the water-filled entrances and not be seen again until evening.

Beaver: Fact or Fiction?

People will tell you as a fact that when a beaver cuts down a tree, he can gauge exactly where it will fall.

But the fact is that, as often as not, the tree only falls partway, with its top entangled in the top of another, so the beaver's work is wasted.

Others will tell you that when a break develops on the dam, the "Boss Beaver" takes charge of the repairs—directing the work of others in the colony.

The fact is: there is no concerted effort—each beaver brings up what he finds handy and puts it where he thinks best.

You may also hear that the beaver uses his wide, flat tail as a trowel to smooth mud into the piles of sticks he's using to build his dam.

The fact is: his tail drags behind him as he works, leaving behind smooth, trowel-like marks. Nothing more.

People who hustle and bustle busily about their work are described as "working like beavers."

Fact is: beavers seldom seem to hustle. They make great changes in their neighborhood, but only a little at a time—a job here and there, with plenty of time off for naps or the search for something to eat.

But one thing beavers do do, is use their tails to give warning of DANGER.

The slap of that wide, flat tail on the water can be heard for a surprising distance.

FIRST EDITION
Library of Congress Cataloging-in-Publication Data
Rounds, Glen, 1906–
Beaver / Glen Rounds. — 1st ed.
p.   cm.
Summary: Describes the physical characteristics, diet, and
nighttime activities of the beaver, an expert swimmer and builder.
ISBN 0-8234-1440-X
1. Beavers—Juvenile literature.   [1. Beavers.]   I. Title.
QL737.R632R66 1999
599.37—DC21   98-28803   CIP   AC